baa cheep squa coo moo
cluck squa oink
coo neigh baa
woof n squeal
duuck Moo
snort ribbit cluck
oink neigh
Oink moo woof
baa quackt
cheep buuuck baa
squeal squawk coo

PATCH of SKY

by Nic Yulo

Dial Books for Young Readers

For Vita,
who started it all

Dial Books for Young Readers
An imprint of Penguin Random House LLC, New York

First published in the United States of America by Dial Books for Young Readers, an imprint of Penguin Random House LLC, 2022

Visit us online at penguinrandomhouse.com.

Library of Congress Cataloging-in-Publication Data is available.

Manufactured in China • ISBN 9780593353844
TOPL

1 3 5 7 9 10 8 6 4 2

Design by Lily Malcom
Text was hand lettered by the artist
The art for this book was created digitally.

Pia and her bestpal, Patches, had always done everything together...

...until
now.

Did you KNOW that pigs
CAN'T SEE the SKY?

Pia just found out too.

Her papa told her while they were feeding the chickens.

But PATCHES is a PIG. And the SKY had been with Pia FOREVER, just like PATCHES.

That's not NOTHING!

That's cuckoo bananas!

When Pia asked WHY, her papa said,
"The way their necks are built, they can't look UP.
Pigs go their WHOLE LIVES without seeing the sky.
NO WAY. NO HOW."

So NOW,
Pia is on a mission.

"You need to see the SKY, Patches! It's BIG and BLUE and SPARKLY. And when you're happy, the clouds float and dance along with you."

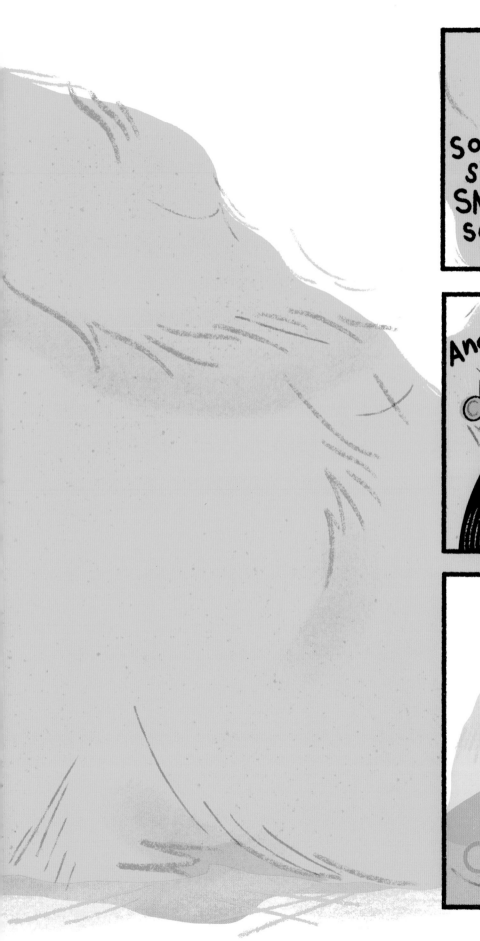

But the only thing THAT does is turn Patches upside down.

His nose still points in the same direction.
(And that direction is not UP.)

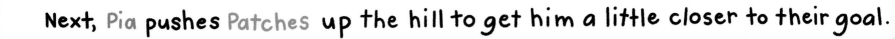

"The sky can be SOFT and DREAMY and help you stay calm when you're scared."

"We need a better angle.
Let's stand on the chicken coop ramp!"

SQUAAWK KKK

But Pia quickly learns that GRAVITY
isn't the only thing that's against her...

...the chickens are too.

"When you're feeling sad,
the sky can be gloomy and gray too.
Just like today."

But then, Pia spots something

FUZZY in the water.

So she digs

SPLOOSH

and digs

until the puddle is deep

enough and wide enough for two.

"Can you see it now?"

SNORT. SQUEEEEEEEE!

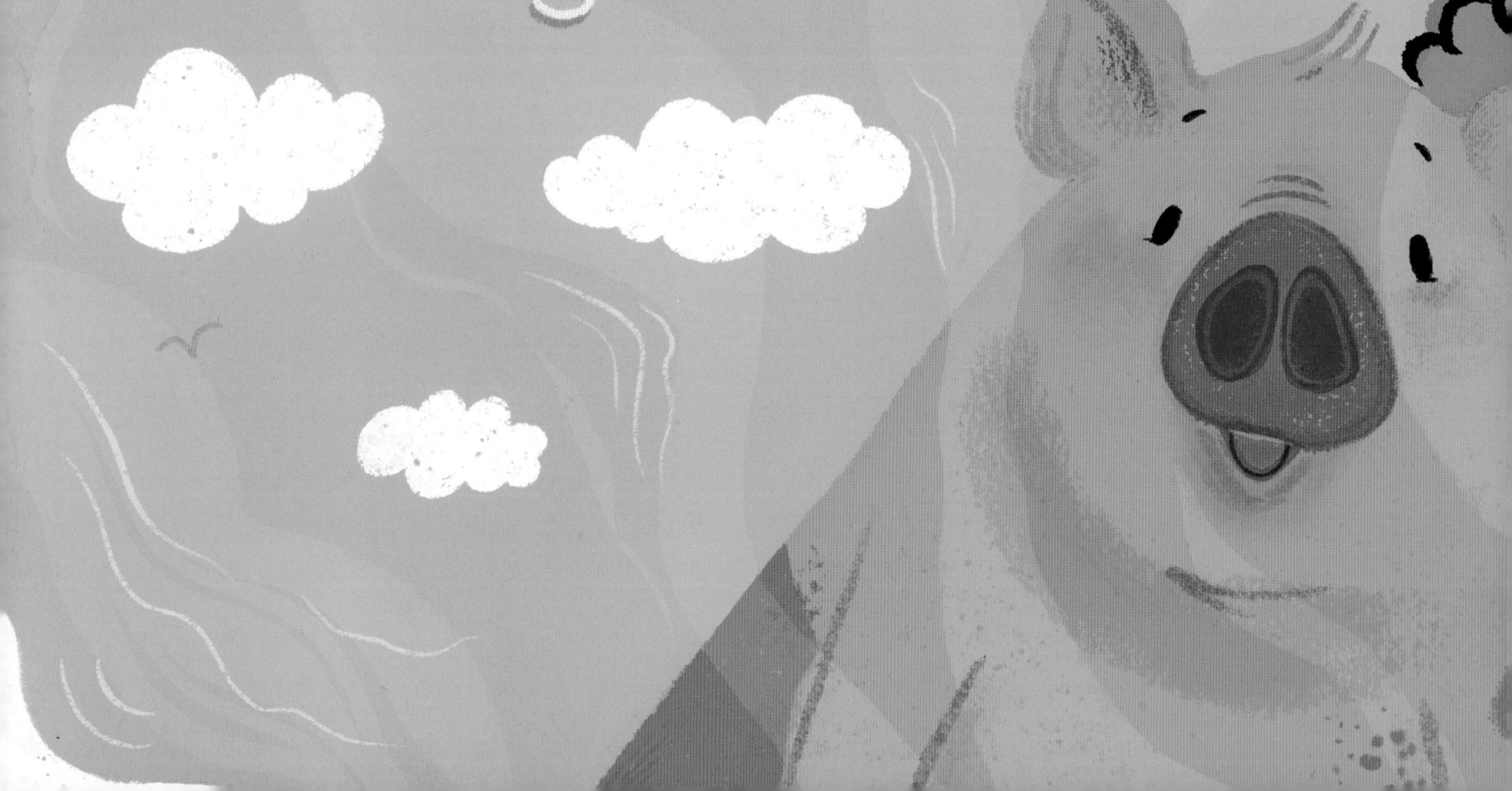

"Papa told me to remember
we're all under the same sky.

"No matter where you are
or how BIG you GROW,
the SKY will ALWAYS
be there for you, Patches.

"And SO WILL I!"

oink!

And so Pia and Patches are on a mission.

Because the sky is BIG and BLUE and SPARKLY and DREAMY and GRAY.

It will change day by day, just like YOU...

...and there's more than enough to SHARE.

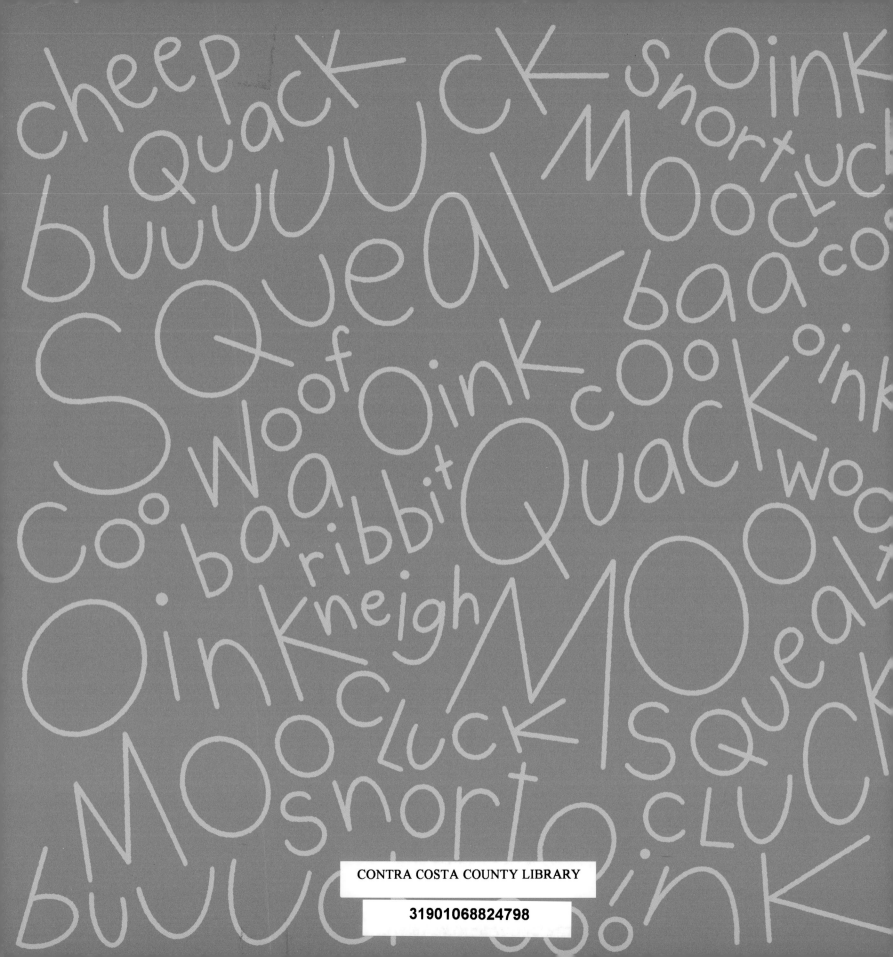